Contents

First edition

© LADYBIRD BOOKS LTD MCMLXXXIV

Animal Poems

chosen by Audrey Daly

Ladybird Books Loughborough

Outside

He's pulling on his boots!
He's going out again —
Out to the world of roots,
The whipping wind and rain,
The stinging sun that tells
On bristles and in blood,
Out to the place of smells,
And things that move, and mud;
Out where, to run a race,
Is not to hit a wall;
Out to the time of chase!
Will he whistle and call?
He's looking for his stick,
He's — Hark! his glorious shout!
I'm coming quick-quick-quick!
We're going out! We're *Out*.

Eleanor Farjeon

The Four Friends

Ernest was an elephant, a great big fellow,
    Leonard was a lion with a six-foot tail,
George was a goat, and his beard was yellow,
    And James was a very small snail.

Leonard had a stall, and a great big strong one,
    Ernest had a manger, and its walls were thick,
George found a pen, but I think it was the wrong
    one,
    And James sat down on a brick.

Ernest started trumpeting, and cracked his manger,
    Leonard started roaring, and shivered his stall,
James gave the huffle of a snail in danger
    And nobody heard him at all.

Ernest started trumpeting and raised such a rumpus,
    Leonard started roaring and trying to kick,
James went a journey with the goat's new compass
    And he reached the end of his brick.

Ernest was an elephant and very well-intentioned,
    Leonard was a lion with a brave new tail,
George was a goat, as I think I have mentioned,
    But James was only a snail.

A A Milne

The Christening

What shall I call
    My dear little dormouse?
His eyes are small,
    But his tail is e-nor-mouse.

I sometimes call him Terrible John,
'Cos his tail goes on –
And on –
And on.
And I sometimes call him Terrible Jack,
'Cos his tail goes on to the end of his back.
And I sometimes call him Terrible James,
'Cos he says he likes me calling him names...

But I think I shall call him Jim,
'Cos I *am* fond of him.

A A Milne

Honey Bear

There was a big bear
Who lived in a cave;
His greatest love
Was honey.
He had twopence a week
Which he never could save,
So he never had
Any money.
I bought him a money box
Red and round,
In which to put
His money.
He saved and saved
Till he got a pound,
Then spent it all
On honey.

Elizabeth Lang

9

The Owl and the Pussy-Cat

The Owl and the Pussy-Cat went to sea
In a beautiful pea-green boat;
They took some honey, and plenty of money,
Wrapped up in a five-pound note.
The Owl looked up to the stars above,
And sang to a small guitar,
'O lovely Pussy! O Pussy, my love,
What a beautiful Pussy you are,
　　You are,
　　You are!
What a beautiful Pussy you are!'

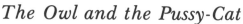

Pussy said to the Owl, 'You elegant fowl!
How charmingly sweet you sing!
O let us be married! Too long we have tarried;
But what shall we do for a ring?'
They sailed away for a year and a day,
To the land where the Bong-tree grows,
And there in a wood, a Piggy-wig stood,
With a ring at the end of his nose,
    His nose,
    His nose,
With a ring at the end of his nose.

'Dear Pig, are you willing to sell for one shilling
Your ring?' Said the Piggy, 'I will.'
So they took it away, and were married next day
By the Turkey who lives on the hill.
They dined on mince, and slices of quince,
Which they ate with a runcible spoon;
And hand in hand, on the edge of the sand,
They danced in the light of the moon,
    The moon,
    The moon,
They danced in the light of the moon.

Edward Lear

Dachshund

Sharp nose raised,
He centipedes by,
Three dogs long...
And half-a-dog high –

A round, smooth hull
For his tail to steer,
And two little squat legs
Bringing up the rear.

Clive Sansom

13

Pensioners

They lean to each other, those two,
The old grey friend and the brown,
Where summer paddocks run down
To the valley that holds the town,
Distant, and faintly blue.

Dreaming of thick green grass
(But not of the cold)
When autumn clouds have rolled
Over the range, to fold
The land in mist as they pass.

Dreaming of no delight
More than they know
Where clover crops are snow
Thick where rich pastures grow,
And all their own and their right.

They lean to each other, those friends,
The old brown horse and the grey,
Knowing the close of day
Brings stars to light the way,
And peace when the twilight ends.

Irene Gough

Our Little Calf

Our little calf is woollier
Inside her ears is soft with fur
She isn't playful any more.

She used to kick her little heels
And run across the summer fields.

Now all she does is stand and stare
Across the stubble, wondering where
Her good grass dinner's gone and why
That white is falling from the sky.

You silly thing, it's winter now.
What you are looking at is snow.

But Spring will come, and Summer too.

And when the world is warm again
And fields are green, d'you know what then?
You'll be our cow!

Dorothy Aldis

The Polar Bear

The Polar Bear is unaware
    Of cold that cuts me through:
For why? He has a coat of hair.
    I wish I had one too!

H Belloc

The Lion

The Lion, the Lion, he dwells in the waste,
He has a big head and a very small waist;
But his shoulders are stark, and his jaws they are
grim,
And a good little child will not play with him.

H Belloc

The Tiger

The Tiger on the other hand, is kittenish and mild,
He makes a pretty playfellow for any little child;
And mothers of large families (who claim to common
sense)
Will find a Tiger well repay the trouble and expense.

H Belloc

The Dog

The truth I do not stretch or shove
When I state the dog is full of love.
I've also found, by actual test,
A wet dog is the lovingest.

Ogden Nash

My Dog

His nose is short and scrubby;
    His ears hang rather low;
And he always brings the stick back,
    No matter how far you throw.

He gets spanked rather often
    For things he shouldn't do,
Like lying-on-beds, and barking,
    And eating up shoes when they're new.

He always wants to be going
    Where he isn't supposed to go.
He tracks up the house when it's snowing —
    Oh, puppy, I love you so.

Marchette Chute

A Kitten

He's nothing much but fur
And two round eyes of blue,
He has a giant purr
And a midget mew.

He darts and pats the air,
He starts and cocks his ear,
When there is nothing there
For him to see and hear.

He runs around in rings
But why we cannot tell;
With sideway leaps he springs
At things invisible —

Then half-way through a leap
His startled eyeballs close,
And he drops off to sleep
With one paw on his nose.

Eleanor Farjeon

21

The Squirrel

Whisky, frisky,
Hippity hop,
Up he goes
To the tree top!

Whirly, twirly
Round and round,
Down he scampers
To the ground.

Furly, curly
What a tail!
Tall as a feather,
Broad as a sail!

Where's his supper?
In the shell.
Snappity, crackity,
Out it fell!

Unknown

The Walrus and the Carpenter

The sun was shining on the sea,
    Shining with all his might:
He did his very best to make
    The billows smooth and bright –
And this was odd, because it was
    The middle of the night.

The moon was shining sulkily,
    Because she thought the sun
Had got no business to be there
    After the day was done –
'It's very rude of him,' she said,
    'To come and spoil the fun!'

The sea was wet as wet could be,
    The sands were dry as dry.
You could not see a cloud, because
    No cloud was in the sky:
No birds were flying overhead –
    There were no birds to fly.

The Walrus and the Carpenter
    Were walking close at hand:
They wept like anything to see
    Such quantities of sand:
'If this were only cleared away,'
    They said, 'it would be grand!'

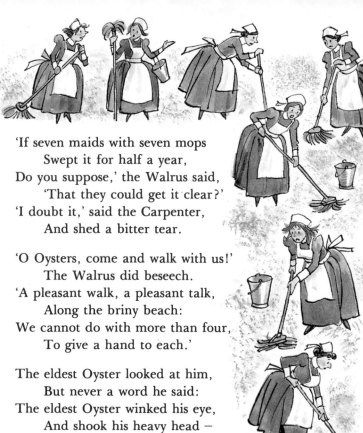

'If seven maids with seven mops
    Swept it for half a year,
Do you suppose,' the Walrus said,
    'That they could get it clear?'
'I doubt it,' said the Carpenter,
    And shed a bitter tear.

'O Oysters, come and walk with us!'
    The Walrus did beseech.
'A pleasant walk, a pleasant talk,
    Along the briny beach:
We cannot do with more than four,
    To give a hand to each.'

The eldest Oyster looked at him,
    But never a word he said:
The eldest Oyster winked his eye,
    And shook his heavy head –
Meaning to say he did not choose
    To leave the oyster-bed.

But four young Oysters hurried up,
    All eager for the treat:
Their coats were brushed, their faces washed,
    Their shoes were clean and neat –
And this was odd, because you know,
    They hadn't any feet.

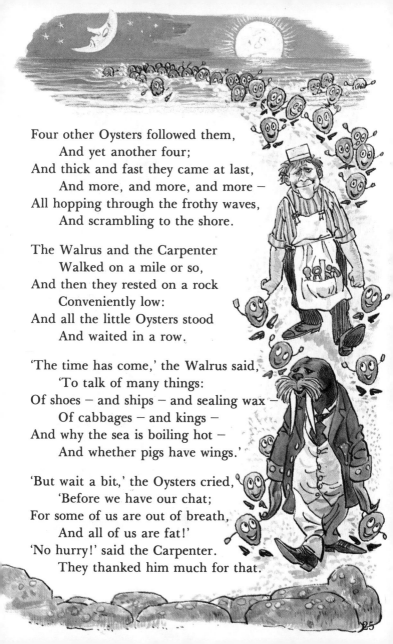

Four other Oysters followed them,
    And yet another four;
And thick and fast they came at last,
    And more, and more, and more —
All hopping through the frothy waves,
    And scrambling to the shore.

The Walrus and the Carpenter
    Walked on a mile or so,
And then they rested on a rock
    Conveniently low:
And all the little Oysters stood
    And waited in a row.

'The time has come,' the Walrus said,
    'To talk of many things:
Of shoes — and ships — and sealing wax —
    Of cabbages — and kings —
And why the sea is boiling hot —
    And whether pigs have wings.'

'But wait a bit,' the Oysters cried,
    'Before we have our chat;
For some of us are out of breath,
    And all of us are fat!'
'No hurry!' said the Carpenter.
    They thanked him much for that.

25

'A loaf of bread,' the Walrus said,
    'Is what we chiefly need:
Pepper and vinegar besides
    Are very good indeed —
Now, if you're ready, Oysters dear
    We can begin to feed.'

'But not on us!' the Oysters cried,
    Turning a little blue.
'After such kindness, that would be
    A dismal thing to do!'
'The night is fine,' the Walrus said,
    'Do you admire the view?

'It was so kind of you to come!
    And you are very nice!'
The Carpenter said nothing but
    'Cut us another slice.
I wish you were not quite so deaf —
    I've had to ask you twice!'

'It seems a shame,' the Walrus said,
    'To play them such a trick.
After we've brought them out so far,
    And made them trot so quick!'
The Carpenter said nothing but,
    'The butter's spread too thick!'

'I weep for you,' the Walrus said:
  'I deeply sympathise.'
With sobs and tears he sorted out
  Those of the largest size,
Holding his pocket-handkerchief
  Before his streaming eyes.

'O Oysters,' said the Carpenter,
  'You've had a pleasant run!
Shall we be trotting home again?'
  But answer came there none —
And this was scarcely odd, because
  They'd eaten every one.

Lewis Carroll

The Wolf

When the pale moon hides and the wild wind wails,
And over the treetops the night hawk sails,
The grey wolf sits on the world's far rim,
And howls: and it seems to comfort him.

The wolf is a lonely soul, you see;
No beast in the wood, nor bird in the tree,
But shuns his path; in the windy gloom
They give him plenty, and plenty of room.

So he sits with his long, lean face to the sky
Watching the ragged clouds go by.
There in the night, alone, apart,
Singing the song of his lone, wild heart.

Far away, on the world's dark rim
He howls, and it seems to comfort him.

Georgia R Durston

28

The Tyger

Tyger! Tyger! burning bright
In the forests of the night,
What immortal hand or eye
Could frame thy fearful symmetry?

In what distant deeps or skies
Burnt the fire of thine eyes?
On what wings dare he aspire?
What the hand dare seize the fire?

And what shoulder, and what art,
Could twist the sinews of thy heart?
And when thy heart began to beat,
What dread hand? And what dread feet?

What the hammer? What the chain?
In what furnace was thy brain?
What the anvil? What dread grasp
Dare its deadly terrors clasp?

When the stars threw down their spears,
And water'd heaven with their tears,
Did he smile his work to see?
Did he who made the Lamb make thee?

Tyger! Tyger! burning bright
In the forests of the night,
What immortal hand or eye,
Dare frame thy fearful symmetry?

William Blake

Puppy and I

I met a Man as I went walking;
We got talking,
Man and I.
'Where are you going to, Man?' I said
    (I said to the Man as he went by).
'Down to the village, to get some bread.
      Will you come with me?' 'No, not I.'

I met a Horse as I went walking;
We got talking,
Horse and I.
'Where are you going to, Horse, today?'
    (I said to the Horse as he went by).
'Down to the village to get some hay.
      Will you come with me?' 'No, not I.'

I met a Woman as I went walking;
We got talking,
Woman and I.
'Where are you going to, Woman, so early?'
    (I said to the Woman as she went by).
'Down to the village to get some barley.
      Will you come with me?' 'No, not I.'

I met some Rabbits as I went walking;
We got talking,
Rabbits and I.
'Where are you going in your brown fur coats?'
    (I said to the Rabbits as they went by).
'Down to the village to get some oats.
    Will you come with us?' 'No, not I.'

I met a Puppy as I went walking;
We got talking,
Puppy and I.
'Where are you going this nice fine day?'
    (I said to the Puppy as he went by).
'Up in the hills to roll and play.'
    'I'll come with you, Puppy,' said I.

A A Milne

When You Talk to a Monkey

When you talk to a Monkey
He seems very wise.

He scratches his head,
And he blinks both his eyes;

But he won't say a word,
He just swings on a rail

And makes a big question mark
Out of his tail.

Rowena Bennett

Tabbies

Tiger and Tim
And Mother Grey
Sleep in the sun
For half the day,
Their tails all under
Their fat cheeks curled
They don't care a button
For all the world.
With their thin gold eyes
And sides so sleek
They look as if
They would sleep a week.

Irene Gough

The Kangaroo

It is a curious thing that you
don't wish to be a kangaroo.
To hop hop hop
and never stop
the whole day long and the whole night too!

To hop across Australian plains
with tails that sweep behind like trains
and small front paws
and pointed jaws
and pale neat coats to shed the rains.

If skies be blue, if skies be grey,
they bound in the same graceful way
into dim space
at such a pace
that where they go there's none to say!

Elizabeth Coatsworth

Missing

Has anybody seen my mouse?

I opened his box for half a minute,
Just to make sure he was really in it,
And while I was looking, he jumped outside!
I tried to catch him, I tried, I tried...
I think he's somewhere about the house.
Has *anyone* seen my mouse?

Uncle John, have you seen my mouse?

Just a small sort of mouse, a dear little brown one,
He came from the country, he wasn't a town one,
So he'll feel all lonely in a London street;
Why, what could he possibly find to eat?

A A Milne

The Firefly

This beast is real, but fabulous;
    An animated spark,
It weaves soft patterns through the night
    And punctuates the dark;

A firework that is soundless,
    By no crude taper lit;
A flame that you can handle —
    If you can capture it!

Edward Lowbury

The Monster

A monster who lives in Loch Ness
Is ten thousand years old, more or less:
 He's asleep all the time –
 Which is hardly a crime:
If he weren't, we'd be in a mess!

Edward Lowbury

A Reproof of Gluttony

The Elephant will eat of hay
Some four and twenty tons a day,
And in his little eyes express
His unaffected thankfulness
That Providence should deign to find
Him food of this delicious kind.
While they that pay for all the hay
Will frequently be heard to say
How highly privileged they feel
To help him make so large a meal.
The Boa Constrictor dotes on goats;
The Horse is quite content with oats,
Or will alternatively pass
A happy morning munching grass.

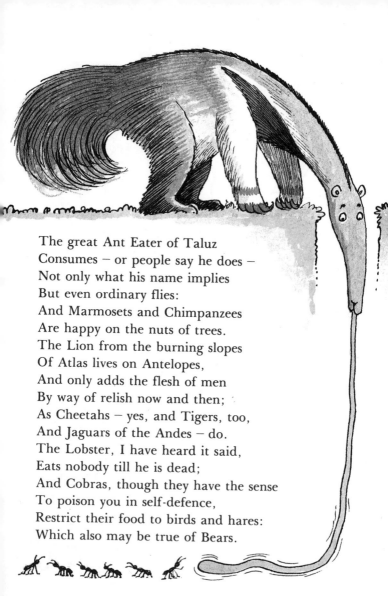

The great Ant Eater of Taluz
Consumes — or people say he does —
Not only what his name implies
But even ordinary flies:
And Marmosets and Chimpanzees
Are happy on the nuts of trees.
The Lion from the burning slopes
Of Atlas lives on Antelopes,
And only adds the flesh of men
By way of relish now and then;
As Cheetahs — yes, and Tigers, too,
And Jaguars of the Andes — do.
The Lobster, I have heard it said,
Eats nobody till he is dead;
And Cobras, though they have the sense
To poison you in self-defence,
Restrict their food to birds and hares:
Which also may be true of Bears.

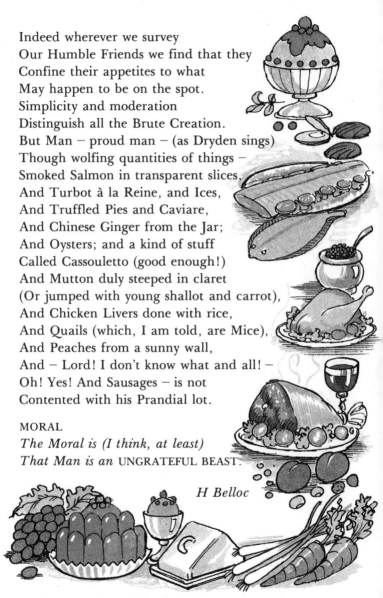

Indeed wherever we survey
Our Humble Friends we find that they
Confine their appetites to what
May happen to be on the spot.
Simplicity and moderation
Distinguish all the Brute Creation.
But Man – proud man – (as Dryden sings)
Though wolfing quantities of things –
Smoked Salmon in transparent slices,
And Turbot à la Reine, and Ices,
And Truffled Pies and Caviare,
And Chinese Ginger from the Jar;
And Oysters; and a kind of stuff
Called Cassouletto (good enough!)
And Mutton duly steeped in claret
(Or jumped with young shallot and carrot),
And Chicken Livers done with rice,
And Quails (which, I am told, are Mice),
And Peaches from a sunny wall,
And – Lord! I don't know what and all! –
Oh! Yes! And Sausages – is not
Contented with his Prandial lot.

MORAL
The Moral is (I think, at least)
That Man is an UNGRATEFUL BEAST.

H Belloc

41

The Sea Gull

The sea gull curves his wings,
The sea gull turns his eyes.
Get down into the water, fish!
(If you are wise.)

The sea gull slants his wings,
The sea gull turns his head.
Get down into the water, fish!
(Or you'll be dead.)

Elizabeth Coatsworth

On a Cat, Ageing

He blinks upon the hearth-rug,
    And yawns in deep content,
Accepting all the comforts
    That Providence has sent.

Louder he purrs and louder,
    In one glad hymn of praise
For all the night's adventures,
    For quiet restful days.

Life will go on for ever,
    With all that cat can wish;
Warmth and the glad procession
    Of fish and milk and fish.

Only – the thought disturbs him –
    He's noticed once or twice,
The times are somehow breeding
    A nimbler race of mice.

Alexander Gray

Acknowledgments

*The compiler and publishers wish to acknowledge
the use of illustrative material as follows: pages 10, 11, 13, 23-7, and 38, Martin Aitchison;
8 and 22, Ian Anderson; 34, Heather Angel; cover, pages 4, 12/13, 14, 19, 20, 21,
and back cover, Tim Clark; 16 and 17, Bruce Coleman Ltd; 29, Margaret Gold;
28, Frank Humphris; 6 and 7, Kathie Layfield; 9, 18, 32, 36, 39, 40, 41, Ken McKie;
37 and 42, Natural History Photographic Agency; 33, Christine Owen;
43, John Paull; 30 and 31, Harry Wingfield.*

*Permission to use copyright poems has been granted as follows:
Dorothy Aldis' 'Our Little Calf' from All Together by Dorothy Aldis,
copyright 1952, copyright renewed 1980 by Roy E Porter, reprinted by permission of
G P Putnam's Sons; Hilaire Belloc's 'The Lion', 'The Polar Bear', 'The Tiger', and
'A Reproof of Gluttony' from Cautionary Verses by Hilaire Belloc.
Copyright 1931 by Hilaire Belloc and renewed 1959 by Eleanor Jebb Belloc,
Elizabeth Belloc, and Hilary Belloc. Reprinted by permission of
Alfred A Knopf, Inc and Gerald Duckworth & Co, Ltd;
Rowena Bennett's 'When You Talk to a Monkey' from The Day is Dancing by
Rowena Bennett. Copyright 1968. Used by permission of Modern Curriculum Press,
Cleveland, Ohio; Marchette Chute's 'My Dog' from Around and About by
Marchette Chute. Copyright 1957, E P Dutton. Reprinted by permission of the author.
Elizabeth Coatsworth's 'The Kangaroo' and 'The Sea Gull' are reprinted with
permission of Macmillan Publishing Company from Summer Green by
Elizabeth Coatsworth. Copyright 1947, 1948 by Macmillan Publishing Company Inc,
renewed 1975, 1976 by Elizabeth Coatsworth Beston; Georgia R Durston's 'The Wolf',
copyright 1969, by permission of Highlights for Children Inc, Columbus, Ohio;
Eleanor Farjeon's 'Outside' and 'A Kitten' from Silver Sand and Snow published by
Michael Joseph, by permission of David Higham Associates Ltd;
Irene Gough's 'Pensioners' and 'Tabbies' from One Sunday Morning Early by
permission of the author; Alexander Gray's 'On a Cat, Ageing', by permission of
Mr John Gray; Elizabeth Lang's 'Honey Bear' from The Book of 1000 Poems by
permission of Bell & Hyman Ltd; Edward Lowbury's 'The Monster' and 'The Firefly'
from Green Magic by permission of the author; A A Milne's 'The Four Friends',
'The Christening', 'Puppy and I', and 'Missing' from When We Were Very Young
published by Methuen Children's Books, by permission of
Associated Book Publishers Ltd, E P Dutton & Elsevier Book Operations, New York,
and the Canadian publishers McLelland & Stewart Ltd, Toronto;
Ogden Nash's 'The Dog', copyright 1962 by Ogden Nash, from
Everyone But Thee and Me and I Wouldn't Have Missed It
(Andre Deutsch 1983), by permission of Andre Deutsch and Little, Brown & Co;
Clive Sansom's 'Dachshund' from The Golden Unicorn (Methuen) by
permission of David Higham Associates Ltd.*